For best friends everywhere
and especially for
my husband Philippe Gonnet (SB)
my wife Helena Harrison (HH)

First published in Hong Kong in 2007 by:

Auspicious Times Limited
Room 511B, 5th Floor,
Hing Wai Centre,
7 Tin Wan Praya Road,
Tin Wan, Hong Kong
Tel: +852 9835 8074
E-mail: enquiries@auspicioustimes.com
Website: www.auspicioustimes.com

3rd edition published December 2009
2nd edition published November 2008
This edition published November 2010

Designed by e5
Produced by Macmillan Production (Asia) Ltd
Tracking Code CP-11/10
Printed in Guandong Province China
This book is printed on paper made from well-managed sustainable forest sources.

ISBN: 978-988-18882-6-6

THE TALE OF
CHESTER CHOI

Written by
Sarah Brennan

Illustrated by
Harry Harrison

OYSTER
龙
SAUCE

There was a Chinese dragon
His name was Chester Choi
When Chester Choi grew hungry
He'd eat a little boy
Though sometimes in the evening
When all was dark and quiet
He'd eat a little girl instead
To brighten up his diet.

Now parents hated Chester
They didn't understand
That dragons must eat dinner too
With tasty kids to hand.
They thought that he was evil
And tried to find his lair
But Chester, being magical,
Was neither here nor there.

So Chester Choi grew fatter
And little kids grew few
The townsfolk lived in constant fear
The beast would strike anew.
They hid their children nightly
In cupboards, drawers and vats
Or rolled them up in carpets
Or covered them in mats.

Yet always Chester found them
No matter where they hid
He'd shove them in a cookie jar
And quickly slam the lid.
Then silently, on tiptoe,
He'd creep outside the door
Then tuck the jar beneath his arm
And off away he'd soar.

He'd take them to a magic cave
Invisible and deep
High up a misty mountainside
As sheer as it was steep
And there he'd take the lid off
He'd tip the children out
Then sprinkle them with oyster sauce
And pop them in his mouth.

One cold and windy evening
As Chester ventured out
He felt a tiny prickling
Of loneliness and doubt.
The children that he gobbled,
While tasty nonetheless,
Appeared to be more fun alive
Than dead he must confess.

He'd seen them in their playrooms
Engrossed with all their toys
Their faces lit with laughter
Their laughter filled with joy.
He'd watched them hug their playmates
Whenever they were sad –
The hugs that Chester never knew
When he was just a lad.

He thought about his childhood
With neither mum nor dad
Nor any other dragons
To grin when he was glad.
He thought about his magic cave
So empty, dark and bare
The sort of home you live in when
There's no one else to care.

And, suddenly, a teardrop
Came rolling down his face
It rattled down his scaly cheek
And started gaining pace
It wobbled for a moment
Then slipped beneath his jaw
And, with a noisy splatter,
Went dashing to the floor.

The dragon was astounded!
He hadn't cried for years!
He heaved a mighty dragon sob –
And then collapsed in tears
They formed a salty torrent
Which ran down to the sea

And swept away the towns

where Chester hunted for his tea.

Such rotten luck for Chester
So lonely, so forlorn,
And now, thanks to a teardrop,
His dinners were all gone.
It really was unreasonable
It wasn't fair nor right
He set his jaw with grim resolve –
His luck would change tonight.

Next time he stole a jarful
Of little girls or boys
He'd give them heaps of cuddles
And lots of lovely toys.
Delicious drinks they'd guzzle
On yummy food they'd sup
They'd laugh and play for hours and hours –
And *then* he'd eat them up!

Now far beneath the mountain
Beside the rolling sea
There lived a little urchin
Whose name was Jimmy Lee.
Poor Jimmy was an orphan
His Mum and Dad were dead
And no–one cared for Jimmy so
He cared for him instead.

He woke himself each morning
He made himself his bed
He fed himself his breakfast
He locked his little shed
Then out along the seashore
Come sleet or hail or shine
Young Jimmy would go fishing with
His trusty rod and line.

Young Jim caught sharks for dinner

And lobsters by the pail

He'd tied an octopus in knots

And wrestled with a whale

He'd surfed down giant tsunamis
On the vast South China Sea

Then battled wicked pirates on
His way back home for tea.

So there, down by the seashore,
Lived Jimmy Lee the Brave
And there, up on the mountain,
Lived Chester in his cave.
One tiny, tough and fearless
One hungry, sad and vexed

I wonder if my readers
Can guess what happened next?

It was a stormy evening
The wind blew wet and wild
The lightning flashed as Chester Choi
Went hunting for a child.
He plied the hills and valleys
In search of busy town
But not a house was standing
Where the flood had thundered down.

He flew along the coastline
He searched the rocky bay
He flapped across the beaches
Where the children used to play.
But all was dark and empty
With not a child in view
And as the thunder rumbled
Chester's tummy rumbled too.

But just as day was dawning
And Chester turned for bed
He flew around a corner –
And spotted Jimmy's shed.
He tiptoed to the window
And took a glance around...
Jim didn't know what hit him
When the cookie jar came down!

When Jimmy woke next morning
Inside the magic cave
His captor grinned in welcome
He waved a cheery wave
Then stuffed him full of egg tarts,
Dim sum and lemon tea,
And lots of grown–up goodies
Kids *never* get to see.

They played with Chinese chequers
Fought aliens from Mars
They raced around on rollerblades
Pretending they were cars.
They kicked around a football
Played hockey, darts and dice
They'd neither of them had such fun
Nor had a friend so nice.

Then...Chester's tummy grumbled
His eyes grew mean, he crept
On tiptoe to the cupboard
Where the oyster sauce was kept.
Young Jim played in the corner
He didn't have a clue
What Chester Choi was planning
Or so Chester thought... do you?

Jim grabbed a fluffy feather
He prickled Chester's nose
He poked at Chester's tummy
He jiggled Chester's toes
He tickled Chester's armpits
And underneath his chin
Poor Chester couldn't help it –
He simply had to grin.

The grin grew to a giggle
The giggle to a laugh
The laughter to a loud guffaw
Which doubled him in half
His legs and arms went wobbly
His claws went skittering past
Jim quickly cast his fishing line...
And Chester Choi was trussed!

Snort fiery flames in anger?
Blow clouds of smoke and hide?

Now what do mighty dragons
Unused to being beat
Do when kids like Jimmy Lee
Tie up their hands and feet?

That's not what Chester Choi did –
He huddled up and *cried*.

"I'm *sorry* I ate children!
I'm sorry I was bad!
I'm sorry I scared mums and dads
And made them cross and sad!
I wish the kids I've eaten
Could be alive again
But most of all, I *really wish*
I had a proper friend!"

Young Jimmy was a kind child
He saw the tears were true
He firmly told the dragon
"Here's what we're going to do –
You're going to sit and wait here
I'm going to go to sea
But I'll be back this evening
With something for your tea."

And sure enough that evening
Young Jimmy Lee came back
Heaving a massive snapper
In a tattered hessian sack.
He brought a little cooker,
A steamer, pan and wok
And ginger, rice and scallions
Stuffed in a purple sock.

The dragon watched in silence
As Jimmy washed and sliced
And scaled and cleaned and gutted
And chopped and peeled and diced.
The steamer was all ready -
Onto the wok it went
And Chester sighed in rapture
When he smelt the wondrous scent.

That night, a mighty dragon
Was fed a humble fish
He'd never known such flavours
Could come out of a dish.
He made a vow to Jimmy

"I'll never, ever eat
A little boy or girl again –
Not even for a treat!"

So Jimmy Lee untied him
They hugged and kissed with glee
And Chester left his gloomy cave
To live with Jimmy Lee.
And there they stayed together
Forever and a day
And towns were built, the people smiled
And kids came out to play.

Sarah Brennan

Sarah Brennan is the author of the popular Dirty Story series and of the best-selling Chinese Calendar Tales, all illustrated by Harry Harrison. Born in Tasmania, Australia, she grew up on the slopes of Mount Wellington surrounded by bush animals, goats and exotic poultry. She also played the bagpipes (at the very bottom of the garden) and wrote lots of stories and poems which she kept in a big pink plastic bag! Sarah worked for ten years as a medical lawyer in London before moving to Hong Kong in 1998. She is also the author of the seditiously naughty parenting advice manual *Dummies for Mummies: What to Expect When You're Least Expecting.* Sarah lives in Hong Kong with her French husband, two daughters and an opinionated cocker spaniel, visiting China, Singapore, the UK and Australia on a regular basis.

Visit Sarah Brennan's funny and fabulous website at www.sarah-brennan.com.
You can follow Sarah's blog on http://sarahbrennanblog.wordpress.com.

Harry Harrison

Robert Harrison, nicknamed "Harry", grew up with a Dad in the air force, so he lived in lots of different places including Singapore and Libya before settling down in West London.
As a boy, Harry loved insects, exploring, climbing trees, making dens and playing war, but he didn't like sport! He has been drawing for as long as he can remember, but he's never had any formal art training.

Harry worked as a freelance illustrator in Sydney and London before settling in Hong Kong, where he became the iconic *Harry*, political cartoonist for the *South China Morning Post*. He is also a regular contributor to The Guardian, the Wall Street Journal, Time magazine, the International Finance Review and the Far Eastern Economic Review. He lives with his wife, son, daughter and restlessly senile cat on Lamma Island in Hong Kong.

See more of Harry Harrison's wild and wacky illustrations on http://www.flickr.com/photos/harryharrisonillos.

The Dragon in Chinese Mythology

Dragons, or *Lung* in Mandarin, are hugely important in Chinese mythology, turning up in the arts, literature, architecture and songs for thousands of years. Records of Chinese dragons have been found which pre-date writing in China! They are a symbol of wisdom, power and good luck and, unlike their Western cousins, are usually seen as kind and well-meaning (except, of course, when they're eating children!). Chinese dragons control the rain, rivers, lakes and seas, and terrible floods can occur when a mortal upsets a dragon (or makes him cry like Chester!). They are said to have 117 scales, 81 being *yang* (or good) and 36 being *yin* (or bad), and are usually depicted with four toes. Only Imperial dragons are allowed five toes, and in olden days, people who drew five toes on an ordinary Chinese dragon had their heads chopped off as punishment!